When Spring Comes

by NATALIE KINSEY-WARNOCK

illustrated by STACEY SCHUETT

Dutton Children's Books · New York

The art is acrylic and pastel on gessoed paper.

LIBRARY OF CONGRESS CATALOGING-IN-PUBLICATION DATA

Kinsey-Warnock, Natalie.
When spring comes/by Natalie Kinsey-Warnock;
illustrated by Stacey Schuett.—1st ed.
p. cm.
Summary: A child, living on a farm in the early 1900s,
describes some of the activities that mark the approach of spring.
ISBN 0-525-45008-4
[1. Farm life—Fiction.   2. Spring—Fiction.   3. Family life—Fiction.]
I. Schuett, Stacey, ill.   II. Title.
PZ7.K6293Wh   1993   92-14066   CIP   AC
[E]—dc20

Published in the United States 1993 by
Dutton Children's Books,
a division of Penguin Books USA Inc.
375 Hudson Street, New York, New York 10014

Designed by Joseph Rutt

Printed in Hong Kong
FIRST EDITION

10 9 8 7 6 5 4 3 2 1

For my mother, Louise Rowell Kinsey
                        N.K.-W.

For Dad and Ellen
            S.S.

When spring comes,
we'll gather sweet sap from the sugar bush,
and Papa will stay up all night to boil it down.

I'll pack the snow by the sugarhouse door.
Mama will pour the hot syrup, making swirls on the snow,
and we'll eat the waxy candy
with Grandma's sweet milk doughnuts and sour pickles.

When spring comes, Canada geese will fly north,
honking a long, sad song,
and the music of tree frogs will fill the night.

As the days get warmer,
Mama will put away my long underwear
and my shoes, to save them for best.

Jasmine and I will wade in the brook
and try to catch tadpoles
while minnows nibble my toes.

Papa will take me fishing at Willoughby Falls,
where silvery trout leap upstream to spawn.
He'll show me bobcat tracks in the mud,
and the path where otters slide down the riverbank.

Grandma and I will walk in the woods,
gathering fiddlehead ferns.
We'll dig through the leaves for wild onions,
and she'll show me where the trillium
and wild violets grow.

When spring comes, the apple trees will blossom.
The air will be sweet with lilacs,
and I will carry some to lay on Grandpa's grave.

The birds will come home,
robins and bobolinks and noisy crows.
Mama will chase the swallows from the porch,
but they'll swoop and squawk
and build a nest there anyway.

I'll help Papa hitch up the horses.
He'll plow the garden,
and Mama and I will push seeds into earth
that is as dark and moist as chocolate.

When spring comes,
Grandma and I will walk to the high pasture
to pick wild strawberries that glisten like rubies.
Later they'll nestle, all sugary,
on Grandma's rich biscuits.

At milking time,
Jasmine and I will go for the cows,
and then we'll swim in the spring-fed pond.

I'll run barefoot through the fields,

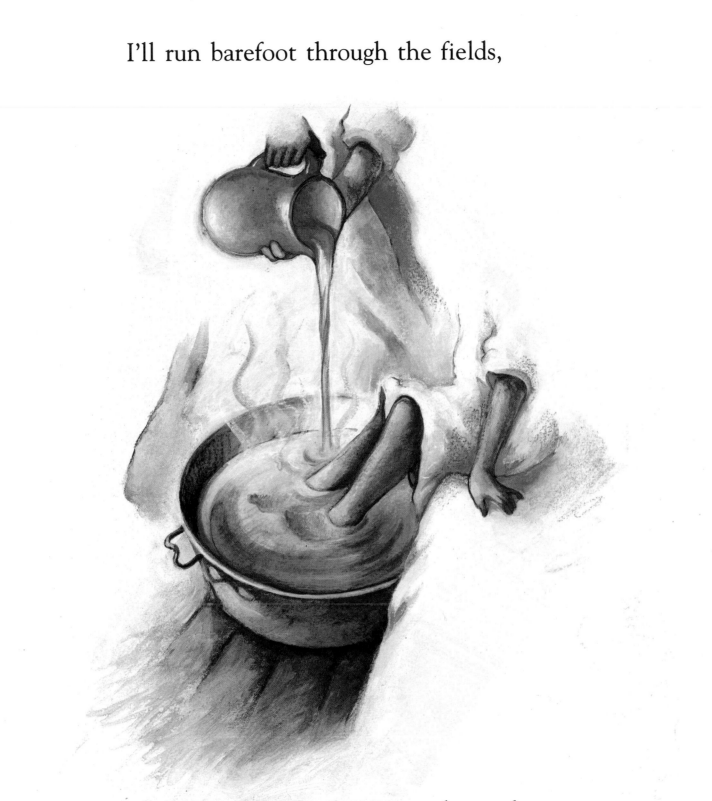

and Mama will make me wash my feet
before I go to bed.

But now I hear the jingle of bells
and run to pull on my woollens.

Papa is on the snow roller,
driving our team of black Morgans.
I love to ride with him
while he packs the roads all smooth and slick.

After supper, he takes me on a sleigh ride.
We swoop down the hill in the silvery light,
and sparks, like stars, stream from the runners.

Papa peers into the great black sky.
He shows me Orion, Cygnus, and the Charioteer,
and I wonder . . .

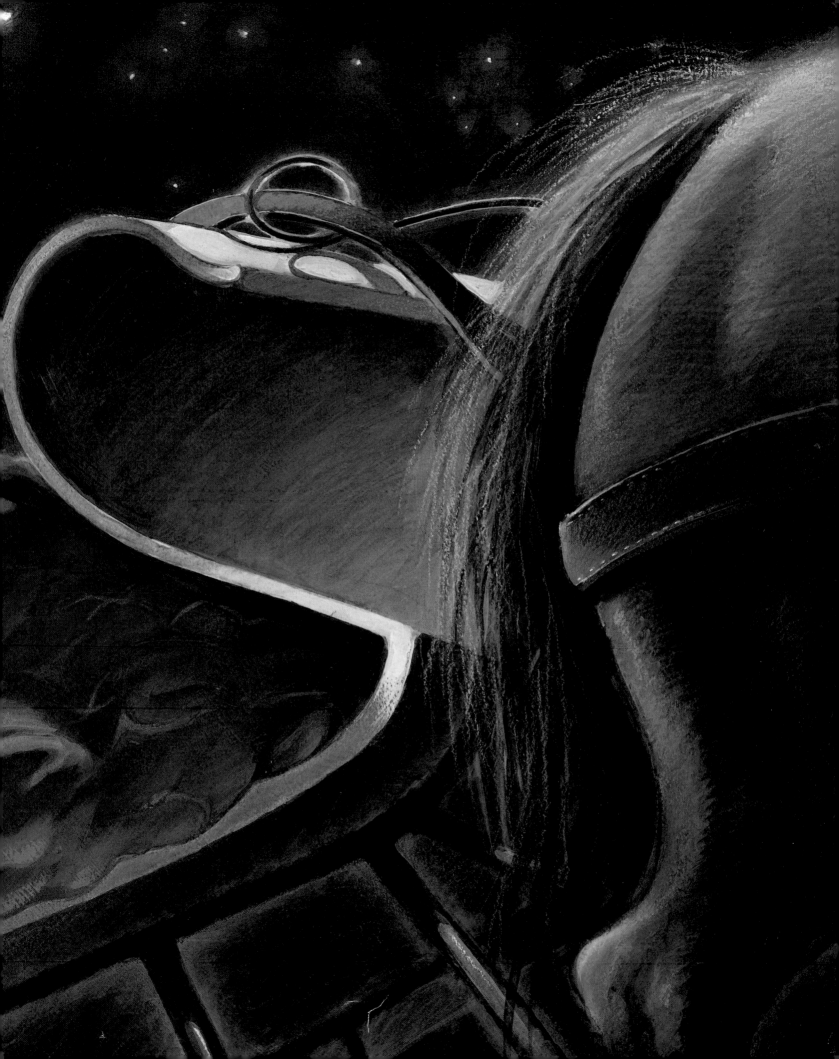

when spring comes,
will the stars be as bright,
the air as sharp and chill,
the night as dark and wonderful . . .

as now?